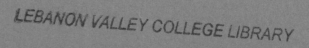

Mouse in the House

John and Ann Hassett

Houghton Mifflin Company Boston 2004

Walter Lorraine Books

For Sammie

Walter Lorraine ⟨wr⟩ Books

Copyright © 2004 by John and Ann Hassett

www.houghtonmifflinbooks.com

Library of Congress Cataloging-in-Publication Data

Hassett, John.
  Mouse in the house / John and Ann Hassett.
     p. cm.
"Walter Lorraine books."
Summary: When Nana Quimby is upset by the mouse in the house, Father
gets an owl, which also upsets Nana, so Mother gets a dog . . . until the
family ends up with an elephant in the house.
  ISBN 0-618-35317-8
[1. Animals—Fiction. 2. Grandmothers—Fiction. 3.
Orderliness—Fiction.] I. Hassett, Ann (Ann M.) II. Title.
  PZ7.H2785Mr 2004
  [E]—dc22
                                                            2003014784

ISBN 0-618-35317-8

Printed in Singapore.
TWP 10 9 8 7 6 5 4 3 2 1

Mouse in the House

One day a family of five moved into a messy old house.

Sister skipped off to collect flies in the attic.

Brother dug in the cellar for bones.

Mother noticed how nicely the cobwebs hid the dirt.

Father carried in Nana Quimby's rocking chair.

And then he took a nap on the floor.

Nana Quimby heard a small scurrying in the walls.
"Eeek — a mouse!" cried Nana Quimby.
"I cannot have a mouse in the house."

She woke Father.
He rang the pet shop on the telephone.
He ordered an owl.

With an owl in the house,
the mouse ran away
to a cheese factory.
Father gave the owl
a bowl of onions for a job well done
and went back to his nap.

But Father's snoring bothered the owl.
The owl flew through the house hooting
and bumping into things.
The owl stared at Nana Quimby
with round owly eyes.
"Eeek!" cried Nana Quimby.
"I cannot have an owl in the house."

Mother rang the pet shop
on the telephone.
She ordered a dog.
With a dog in the house,
the owl flew away
to a hollow tree in the woods.
Mother gave the dog
a jelly donut for a job well done.

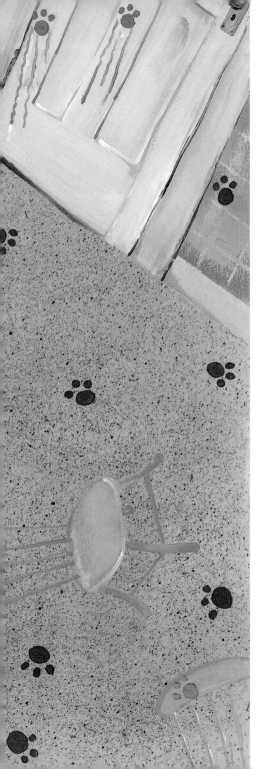

But the dog had fleas.
The dog quarreled with
a skunk under the porch.
The dog thought Nana Quimby
was a burglar.
"Eeek!" cried Nana Quimby,
holding her nose.
"I cannot have a dog in the house."

Brother rang the pet shop
on the telephone.
He ordered an alligator.
With an alligator in the house,
the dog ran away with the mailman.
Brother gave the alligator
a lollipop for a job well done.

But the alligator
swam in the bathtub.
The alligator liked to have
his belly rubbed.
The alligator swallowed
Nana Quimby's shoe.
"Eeek!" cried Nana Quimby.
*"I cannot have
an alligator in the house."*

Sister rang the pet shop
on the telephone.
She ordered a tiger.
With a tiger in the house,
the alligator ran away
to a duck pond in the park.
Sister gave the tiger
buttered toast for a job well done.

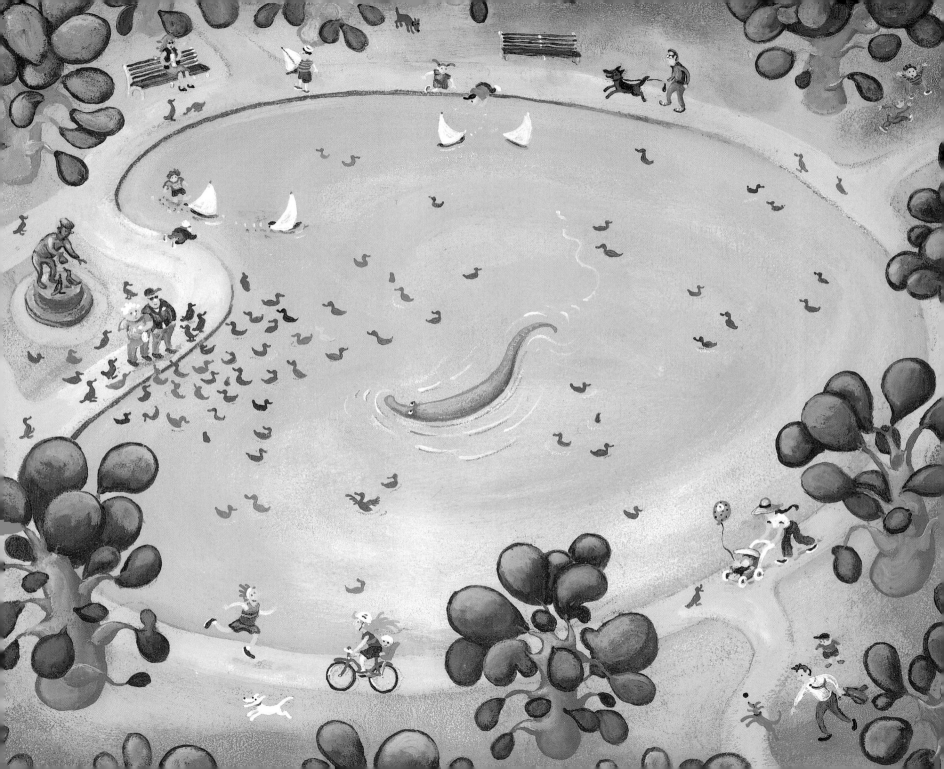

But the tiger got stuck up in a tree. The tiger stole milk. The tiger thought Nana Quimby looked like lunch.

"Eeek!" cried Nana Quimby. "I cannot have a tiger in the house."

Father got up from the floor.
He yawned and rang the pet shop
on the telephone.
He ordered an elephant.
With an elephant in the house,
the tiger ran away to a circus.
Father gave the elephant
a cold glass of root beer
for a job well done.

But the elephant
uprooted a tree
in the yard.
The elephant
marched through
the house like
an earthquake.
The elephant
bumped
Nana Quimby's
rocking chair—
and broke it
all to pieces.

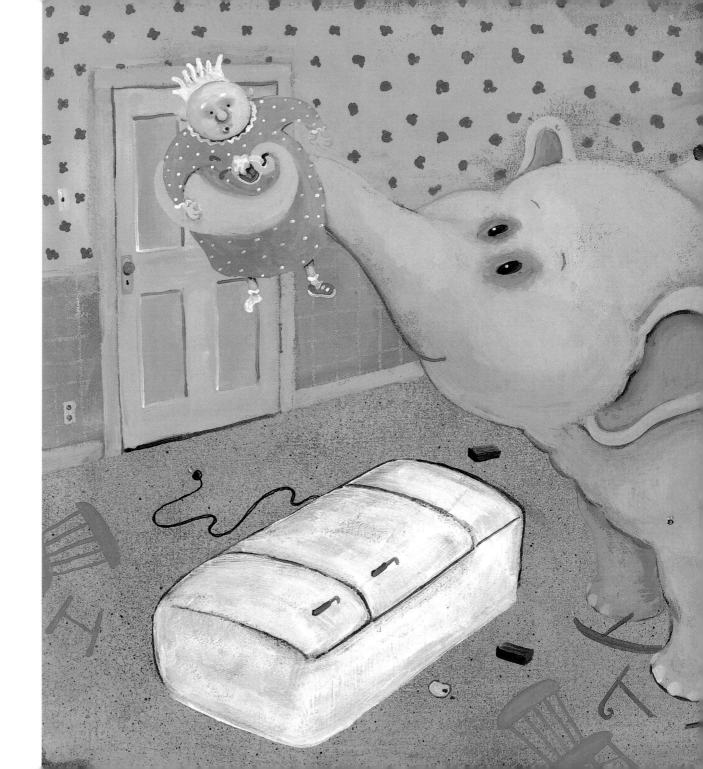

"Enough!" said Nana Quimby.
"I cannot have an elephant in the house."
Nana Quimby rang the pet shop.
She ordered a mouse.
With a mouse in the house,
the elephant ran away
to a peanut farm in the country.

Nana Quimby gave the mouse
a crumb of cheese for a job well done.
Then she rang a taxicab
on the telephone and ran away
to live with her cousin in Florida.